A Promise Is a Promise

A Promise Is a Promise

Florence Parry Heide

illustrated by Tony Auth

CANDLEWICK PRESS
CAMBRIDGE, MASSACHUSETTS

George was a very lucky boy.

Just that week, his father had said,

"You're a very lucky boy, George."

"Your father is right, George," said George's mother. "You have everything a boy could want."

"Well, I don't have a pet," said George. "I'm the only kid in town who doesn't have a pet. I'm probably the only kid in the whole *world* who doesn't have a pet."

"That's ridiculous," said George's father.

"I'll say," said George.

"Oh, dear," said George's mother. "I wouldn't want him to be the only boy in the whole *world* who didn't have a pet."

"So, can I have a pet?" asked George.

His father sighed. "All right, George. You may have a pet."

So George went to look for a pet.

That afternoon, George said to his mother and father,
"I have a pet, and his name is Oliver. I'll bring him in."

George brought in a very large, very shaggy dog.
The dog jumped on George's father and knocked
him down.

"Oh, dear," said George's mother.

"Take him back," said George's father. "Take him back and get a pet that doesn't jump UP on people. Or SHED," he said, brushing himself off.

"Or EAT too much," said George's mother. "He'd eat us out of house and home. And get a pet that doesn't have to be let in and out and taken for walks, dear."

"Jeepers," said George. "Come on, Oliver."

The next day, George said to his mother,
"I have a pet
and it doesn't jump up on people
and it doesn't shed
and it doesn't eat too much
and it doesn't have to be let in and out
and it doesn't have to be taken out on walks
and his name is Philip."

"That's nice, dear," said George's mother.
"Your father will be so pleased."

"This is Philip," said George. "Phoebe is around here somewhere too. Maybe she went to check on her babies."

"Take Philip back and take Phoebe back,"
said George's mother.

"And take the babies back.
NOW!"

"Gee whiz," said George. "You *said* I could have a pet."

"Nothing that scampers," said George's mother.
"And nothing that multiplies."

"*Everything* multiplies," said George.
"Otherwise there wouldn't *be* anything."
"Nothing that multiplies *much,*"
 said George's mother.

"There's Phoebe now,"

she added in a very loud voice.

"Okay, okay," said George.

"You don't have to get so excited."

The next day, George came into the living room.

"I have a new pet," said George,

"and it doesn't jump up on people

and it doesn't shed

and it doesn't have to be let in and out

and it doesn't have to be taken on walks

and it doesn't scamper

and it doesn't multiply much

and her name is Penelope.

She's in the bathtub."

George's mother and father went with George
to see his new pet.

A very large something was in the bathtub.
An enormous something.

George's mother wasn't positive, but she thought it looked very much like a shark.

It WAS a shark.
"Oh, dear," said George's mother.

"This is too much!" said George's father. "Take it back."

"Why?" asked George.
"It doesn't jump up on people and it doesn't—"

"It's too unusual, dear," said George's mother. "And it has such big *teeth*."

"Your mother is right, George," said George's father. "It's too unusual."

George sighed. "You'll never be satisfied. No matter what pet I bring home, you'll find something wrong with it."

"Birds are nice, dear," said George's mother. "They don't jump up on people or shed or—"

"Your mother is right, George," said George's father. "Get a bird."

"Okay, okay," said George. "I'll get a bird. But how do I know you'll let me keep it? You always change your minds."

"Your mother and I PROMISE you may keep a bird," said George's father. "And a promise is a promise."

"Yes, George," said George's mother. "Your father is right. A promise is a promise."

"Well, okay," said George. "Come on, Penelope."

The next day, George came home and said,
"I have a a bird."

"HUBBA, HUBBA," said a voice from the kitchen.

"There's Horatio now," said George.
"I'll bring him in. He loves to visit."

"This is Horatio," said George.

"Well, well," said George's father.

"Mercy!" said George's mother.

"POLLY WANTS A CRACKER," said Horatio.

"Who's Polly?" asked George's mother.

"SHUT UP, YOU BIG BOOB," said Horatio.

"Is he talking to me?" asked
George's mother.

"Take him back, George," said George's father. "Get a bird that doesn't talk."

"YOU'RE A BIG FAT NINCOMPOOP,"

said Horatio.

"Certainly nothing that swears, dear,"

said George's mother.

"Take him back right now, George,"
said George's father.

"But you *promised*," said George.
"And a promise is a promise."

"Yes, dear, you promised,"
said George's mother.

George's father sighed.

"How do things like this happen?"

"HUBBA

"HUBBA," said Horatio.

"GOTCHA!"

"Oh, wow! I guess
a promise really *is* a promise," said George.

To Max, Audrey, Joey, Claire, and
Cecilia Soldenwagner — F. P. H.

To Katie and Emily — T. A.

Text copyright © 2007 by Florence Parry Heide
Illustrations copyright © 2007 by Tony Auth

Library of Congress Catalog-in-Publication Data is available.

Library of Congress Catalog Card Number pending

ISBN 978-0-7636-2285-5

10 9 8 7 6 5 4 3 2 1

Printed in Singapore

This book was typeset in Clichee.
The illustrations were done in ink and watercolor.

Candlewick Press
2067 Massachusetts Avenue
Cambridge, Massachusetts 02140

visit us at www.candlewick.com